LITTLE TIGER PRESS
An imprint of Magi Publications
1 The Coda Centre, 189 Munster Road,
London SW6 6AW
www.littletigerpress.com
This volume copyright © Magi Publications 2007
All rights reserved
ISBN 978-1-84506-614-7
Printed in China
2 4 6 8 10 9 7 5 3 1

Shaggy Dog and the Terrible Itch
David Bedford
Illustrated by Gwyneth Williamson
First published in Great Britain 2001
by Little Tiger Press,
an imprint of Magi Publications
Text copyright © David Bedford 2001
Illustrations copyright © Gwyneth Williamson 2001

Titus's Troublesome Tooth
Linda Jennings
Illustrated by Gwyneth Williamson
First published in Great Britain 2000
by Little Tiger Press,
an imprint of Magi Publications
Text copyright © Linda Jennings 2000
Illustrations copyright © Gwyneth Williamson 2000

Shaggy Dog
and the
Terrible
Itch

David Bedford

Gwyneth Williamson

Shaggy Dog had an itch
on his back. He scratched
against a tree but . . .

his back was
still itchy.

"Will you scratch my back?"
Shaggy Dog asked Mimi the poodle.
"Ugh!" said Mimi, "scratch your
back, *no thank you*! I'm off to the
Poodle Parlour for a wash and trim."

"*I* will scratch your back," said
Farmer Gertie. "But first you
must help me round up my sheep."

The sheep were hiding, and it took ages to find them.

"*Woof woof!*" barked Shaggy Dog. "Come here, sheep, come here *now*!"

At last the sheep were locked in
their pen. Farmer Gertie used her curly
crook to scratch Shaggy Dog's back.

"Ooh!" said Shaggy Dog. "That's
much better."

But as Shaggy Dog walked into town . . .

. . . the itch came back!

Shaggy Dog knocked on
the window of Merv's Cafe.

"Who will scratch the itch from my back?" he asked.

"*I* will," said Merv. "But first you must wash my pots and pans."

Shaggy Dog washed towers
and towers of pots and pans.
Bubbles covered his legs and
got into his mouth, and when
he had finished, his paws
were all wrinkly.

Merv used a long fork to
scratch Shaggy Dog's back.
"Ooh, ooh!" said Shaggy Dog.
"That's much, much better."
But when Shaggy Dog left
the cafe . . .

. . . the itch came back!

Shaggy Dog popped into
Mary Lou's Poodle Parlour.

"Will you scratch the itch from
my back?" asked Shaggy Dog.
   "Okay," said Mary Lou. "But only
if you brush up the fur on the floor."

Shaggy Dog brushed up mountains
and mountains of poodle fur.

Fur got up his nose, and when he had finished, he had fur in his ears and his eyes, too.

Aitchoo!
Aitchoo!
Aitchoo!

he sneezed.

Shaggy Dog shook out all the fur,
and Mary Lou used the poodle brush
to scratch his back.

"Ooh, ooh, ooh!" said Shaggy Dog.
"That's much, much, MUCH better."
But when Mary Lou stopped scratching . . .

. . . the itch came back!

"What can I do?" asked Shaggy Dog.

"Sit in the chair," said Mary Lou.

"I'll wash and trim you."

The bubbly shampoo soothed
Shaggy Dog's back.
  "Ooh, ooh, ooh, OOOH!" said
Shaggy Dog.

The poodle scissors
tickled and went . . .

Snip! Snip! Snip!

"Hee, hee, hee,"
giggled Shaggy Dog.

When Mary Lou had finished
trimming Shaggy Dog's fur . . .

Shaggy Dog felt

wonderful!!

The itch had gone at last . . .

But where did it go?

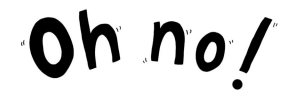

"Oh no!"

Titus's Troublesome Tooth

Linda Jennings and Gwyneth Williamson

Titus the Goat ate everything.
He ate carrots and cabbages.

He ate dandelions
and dock leaves.

He ate prickly,
tickly thistles . . .

And he even ate Farmer Harry's pants and vests off the washing line!

Titus absolutely loved eating —
until one day . . .

. . . he woke up
with a terrible pain.

He didn't want
his breakfast . . .

and he didn't want to munch
and crunch the apples
in the orchard.

He wasn't even tempted to
nibble at Mrs Harry's nightdress.
Titus felt as miserable as . . .

. . . well . . . as miserable as a goat with toothache! He was a very grouchy, grumbly goat indeed.

"That's a troublesome tooth," said Derry the Donkey. "Open your mouth and I'll pull it out with my big, strong teeth."

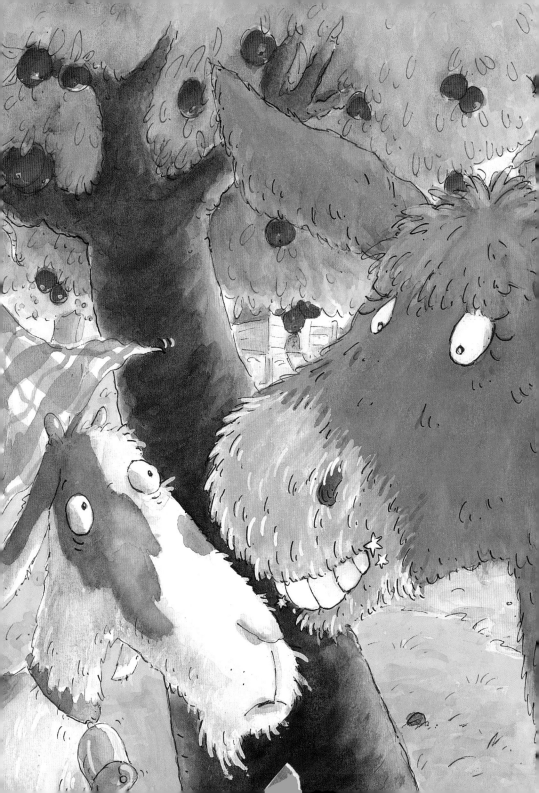

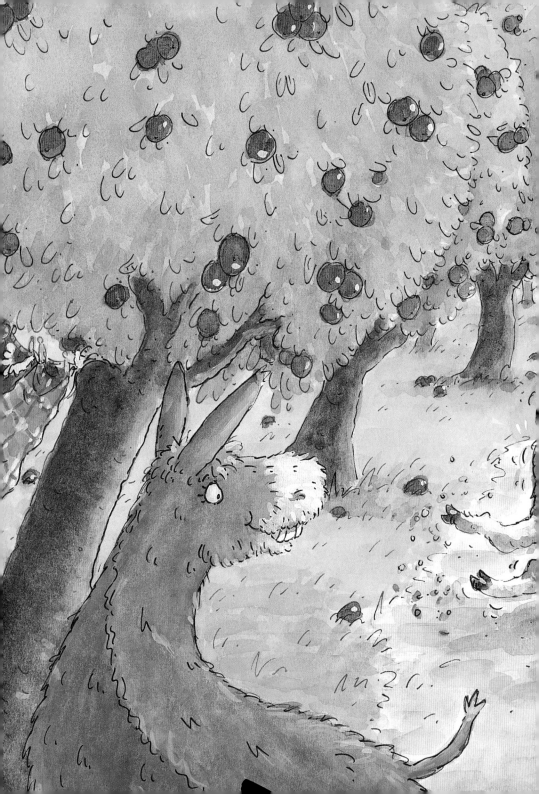

Titus shook from
his horns to the tip
of his tail.

"Ooh-er, no thanks,"
he bleated. He ran
and ran and grouched
and grumbled . . .

. . . until he reached the farmyard.

"That's a troublesome tooth," said
Sadie the Hen. "Open your mouth and
I'll peck it out with my nice, sharp beak."

Titus quivered on all four hooves.
    "Ooh-er, no thanks," he cried.
Titus ran and ran and grouched
and grumbled . . .

. . . until he reached the barn.

"That's a troublesome tooth,"
said Polly the Cat. "Open
your mouth and I'll
scratch it out with
my long, shiny claws."

Titus trembled
from his white beard
to his furry bottom.
"Ooh-er, no
thanks," he shouted.

Titus ran and ran and
grouched and grumbled...

. . . until he reached the meadow.

"That's a troublesome tooth," said Basil
the Bull. "Open your mouth and I'll butt it
out with my hard, curly horns."

All Titus's teeth chattered and
rattled – even the bad one!
   "Ooh-er, no thanks," he sobbed.
Titus ran and ran and grouched
and grumbled . . .

. . . until he reached the duck pond.

"That's a troublesome tooth," said Daphne the Duck. "Open your mouth and I'll tug it out with some duckweed."

Titus shook so much that he nearly fell into the water.

"Ooh-er, no thanks," he yelled.

Titus ran and ran and grouched and grumbled . . .

. . . until he found himself
right back in the farmyard again.

"Don't worry," said Sadie the Hen.
"Farmer Harry will get rid of that
troublesome tooth for you,
because he's called the vet!"

"The vet!"
shouted Titus.

He quivered and he shivered, he
trembled and he shook. His teeth
rattled and chattered – even
the bad one.

"No way do I want
the vet!"

Titus ran and ran . . .

and grouched . . .

and grumbled until . . .

. . . Titus bashed his head
against the fence . . .

And the troublesome
tooth fell out at last!

Wish upon a star with two magical stories from Little Tiger Press!

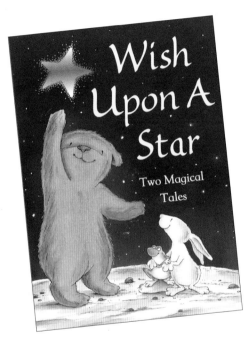

Little Brown Bear wants the perfect present for his mummy's birthday – a beautiful shining star.

Holly wants a tiny, cuddly kitten more than anything else in the world. But soon she gets more than she wished for!

For information regarding the above title or for our catalogue, please contact us:
Little Tiger Press, 1 The Coda Centre, 189 Munster Road, London SW6 6AW
Tel: 020 7385 6333 • Fax: 020 7385 7333
E-mail: info@littletiger.co.uk • www.littletigerpress.com